Table of Contents

Nates Return

Sit on the edge of your seat through this cautionary tale of love, loss, and betrayal.

Nates' Return

Nate is a 17-year-old boy living in the Southwestern United States in the year 1901. It is early fall. He lives with his mother called Miss Nancy. She lost her man in the Spanish-American War. They live on a small farm that provides the veggies, eggs, and milk they need. Nate is a strong lad, but lacking in mental development. He does each task with hard work and persistence until done. He is a good boy that is always respectful and polite to others. He works at the general store at night, doing cleaning and maintenance for $3 a week that he gives to his mother from time to time.

Doc James came calling on Miss Nancy. He always said it was to check on Nate. The truth was he is sweet on Miss Nancy. He'd bring her flowers and such. Nancy looked forward to his visits and always made a tasty meal for him. After supper the two sat on the porch in rocking chairs and chatted while Nancy knitted. Doc James would ask Nancy to marry him on his more recent visits. Nancy would say, with Nate being the way he was, she did not want to be a burden, but she was sweet on him.

The general store Nate worked at was owned by Mr. Johnson and his wife. The Johnson's were fond of Nate and often they would give him a little something to take home to his mother and him. The Johnsons' daughter Marry Lou and Nate were sweet on each other. She is 16-years-old and very pretty and bright. Marry Lou was teaching Nate how to read and write and do math. He did well at it. She taught him how to read from the bible. Marry Lou and Nate spent many hours walking, talking, and sitting on the beach, watching the sunset while holding hands, with a little sparking.

The day came when Nate didn't want to come home. Miss Nancy got really worried as she looked at the time on the coo-coo clock. There was a knock at the door. It was Marry Lou, all upset and crying. Nancy asked her why she was crying.

"You need to come with me. Hurry. Nate is in big trouble." Nancy grabbed her shawl and joined Marry Lou on the buggy toward town. Marry Lou told Nancy what went off. Nate would never hurt anyone, especially the Johnson's, she told Nancy. "Somebody killed Mom and Dad, and folks think Nate did it. They talking of lynching him."

As the women came into town, they saw an angry crowd gathered in front of the jail. The crowd of people were demanding to have Nate turned over to them. The women went from worry and fear to being angry. They jumped off the buggy and walked to the front of the crowd.

The sheriff, standing there said, "You shouldn't be here."

"Where should we be with folks wanting to lynch Nate." The two women followed the sheriff into the jail. Nate sat on bail in his cell with his head in his hands. "Nate, are you ok?" asked his mother. "We here to help you," added Marry Lou. "What happened?"

"I don't know. I don't understand why folks angry with me. What did I do wrong?" said Nate.

The sheriff said, "He killed and robbed the Johnson's."

"That's a lie," stated Marry Lou.

"Damn right it's a lie. Nate is a good Christian man," said Nancy. "Where's your proof?"

"A witness saw him leave the store."

"Nate worked at the store so what's wrong about that?"

"He had blood on him. He says it was to see if the Johnson's were still alive."

"Sheriff, they were my mother and father. Nate didn't need to rob them and he knew it. He was like a son to them," said Marry Lou.

About this time, Doc James came in.

"I'm glad you're here Doc. I don't know what to do. They saying Nate killed the Johnson's. It's not true," said Nancy.

"Try to calm down Miss Nancy. You too Marry Lou."

Doc and the sheriff talked for a few minutes. He returned to the two women. "The sheriff has agreed to let you ladies get Nate out of the cell."

The four of them sat in the office and discussed what happened. Doc asked the deputy to collect Solicitor Brown. He did. Nate, the solicitor, and the women talked about what happened. Nate was confused.

"Why are people so mad at me? What did I do? I don't understand."

The solicitor explained the situation to Nate. "Tell me exactly what happened. Leave nothing out, no matter how unimportant it might seem," he said.

Nate did that.

"So, you went out back of the store to clean up the storage shed. When you finished it was dark and you entered the back door. It was dark as you worked your way across the room and you tripped and fell on Mr. and Mrs. Johnsons' bodies. Shortly after that, Marry Lou came in the store holding a lit lantern. At that time, you realized you were laying on top of Mr. And Mrs. Johnsons' bodies. What happened then?"

"Marry Lou got upset and asked what I did. I told her I tripped over Mr. And Mrs. Johnsons' bodies in the dark. She went to get the sheriff. Some other men came in and said I killed the Johnson's. I told them I didn't. They didn't believe me."

Mr. Brown asked the sheriff where the circuit judge and Texas ranger post was and to send someone to investigate the crime. He also asked that Nate be allowed to go home with his mother. He would be responsible for him. He was told Nate would have to go before the judge to go home. He also said Nates' mother and Marry Lou could stay with him while he was in jail.

The two women took turns staying with Nate. They brought him home cooked meals. Five days later the Texas ranger came to town as well as the judge. The Texas ranger met with Mr. Brown and Marry Lou, as well as Doc James and the sheriff. The judge held hearing and decided Nate could go home with his mother, however, he felt Nate might be safer in jail. "The townspeople being angry, I am concerned for his safety."

The judge met with Mr. Brown in his chambers. He suggested Nate leave the jail after dark to avoid any problems. "I will give you a court order giving him release on bail. I suggest he doesn't venture too far from home and stay out of sight. Your next court date is 30 days from today. Don't let me down. Be there. As far as the townsfolk are concerned, Nate is still in jail."

After interviewing anybody and everybody that knew Nate, and everybody that might know about the murders, and after examining the murder scene, the Texas ranger came to the conclusion that Nate didn't do it. Mr. Brown, the doc, and the Texas ranger spent a lot of time going over the evidence and planning Nates' defense.

When the court date came, Mr. Brown called some of the townspeople to the stand. These people were those outside the jail demanding Nate be turned over to them. Afterwards, he asked the judge for a change of venue because of the townsfolk called to the stand. "Nate can't get a fair trial because the jury pool has been compromised. The judge agreed and moved the trial to the county seat 30 days from that date. He also continued Nates' bail.

The day came to go to the county seat. Nate, Marry Lou, Miss Nancy, Doc James, and Mr. Brown rode together. The Texas ranger would meet them at the county seat. Mr. Brown had asked some of the townsfolk to testify on Nates' general behavior, honesty, and character. Mr. Brown was confident Nate would be found not guilty. At the edge of town, they saw gallows being built. Nate and the rest of them got really worried. Mr. Brown assured them everything would be alright. "We have two days until the trial starts. After we get settled, I will see the prosecutor and feel him out."

The day of the trial, the Texas ranger had not arrived yet. Mr. Brown asked for a one-day continuance to find out why. Again, Nate and the others got worried. Mr. Brown tried to ease their concerns. He was also concerned, but did not let on so. He sent a telegram to the Texas rangers post to ask about the Texas rangers' whereabouts. The answer that came four hours later said he'd been killed during a gun fight in a nearby town. He did leave behind notes concerning Nates' trial. If Mr. Brown wanted the notes, he would have to send someone to get them or he could mail them. Mr. Brown knew he had to get another continuance until the notes arrived. Mr. Brown asked the court for another continuance. The judge got angry. "Where are these notes coming from?"

"They are at the Texas ranger station, three days away by train. They are on their way. They can prove my client is innocent."

"I'll give you a four-day continuance. At that time, notes or not, I will start the trial."

"Yes, sir. Thank you, sir," said Mr. Brown.

Mr. Brown sent the Texas ranger station another telegram about the notes. A response from the ranger station said a ranger with notes will be there in 3 days. Nate and the others were happy and relieved to hear that.

Day four came and went. No ranger and no notes. The next morning in court, Mr. Brown told the judge the ranger had not come yet. The judge started the trial. He revoked Nates' bail and ordered that he be held in jail when not in court.

The prosecutor made Nate out to be a cold-blooded killer and robber. The three men who saw Nate standing over the Johnsons' bodies covered with blood didn't see or hear anyone else. They said "Nate said over and over I didn't do it." They also said they knew he did it. Nate, sitting next to Mr. Brown, kept getting upset. His mother and Marry Lou were upset as well. Mr. Brown told them just to calm down. "Our turn is next."

Mr. Brown questioned the three men. They repeated their testimony. Mr. Brown asked them if they saw Nate kill the Johnson's. They said, "No, but knew he did it."

"How do you know he did it?" said Mr. Brown.

"He was standing over the bodies covered with blood."

Mr. Brown excused the witnesses and asked them to stand in front of the courtroom and put on a blindfold. Then Mr. Brown very quietly asked three women for their purses for a few moments. Mr. Brown put the purses in front of each man.

"Those men have stolen our purses!" the women declared. The three men opened their eyes.

"How do you know they stole your purses?" asked Mr. Brown.

"They laying on the floor in front of the men."

The three men began to deny taking the purses while upset and loud.

"We want to believe you. Can you prove it?" said Mr. Brown.

"Yes," said the men. "We been standing here with our eyes closed."

Mr. Brown asked the three men if maybe they might be wrong about knowing Nate killed the Johnson's.

All three men said yes, they were no longer sure Nate killed the Johnson's. After Mr. Brown gave the ladies back their purses and thanked them for their help, he and his cross exam of the men ended.

The prosecutor called Marry Lou to the stand. He asked her what she saw when she entered the store with the lantern.

"I saw Nate laying on top of my mother and fathers' bodies. He said he didn't do it. I believed him. He had no reason."

After the prosecutor finished with Marry Lou, Mr. Brown questioned her.

"Tell me why you believe Nate didn't kill your parents Marry Lou?"

"Nate is warm-loving and a god-fearing man. He never took something he didn't earn. He is honest and hardworking. My parents loved him like a son and he loved them. I taught him to read with the bible. He never missed Sunday service. He talked of being a pastor someday."

Mr. Brown excused Marry Lou. The prosecutor called the sheriff to the stand. He asked how much Nate had when arrested.

"He had $4.50 in his pocket. Nate told me Mr. Johnson gave him $4.50 for that week because it was his birthday. His regular pay was $3 a week."

"Was the store robbed sheriff?" asked the D.A.

"Yes," said the sheriff. "$500 was missing along with a strong box. Personally, I don't think Nate did it."

"Did what sheriff?" asked the D.A.

"The murder or the robbery. It is just not in the boys' makeup."

"Sheriff, can you say for a fact that Nate did kill the Johnson's?"

"I didn't see the murder so, no," the sheriff answered.

The D.A. rested his case. Mr. Brown asked for a continuance until the next morning. The judge agreed.

Mr. Brown told Nate things were going well and not to worry and get some sleep. I have arranged for your mother and Marry Lou to visit for a while.

The women brought a nice dinner on their visit. They were allowed to visit for one hour with a guard present. The hour went fast. After the women left, Nate sat on his bunk and ran the day court in his mind. He felt more at ease after Mr. Brown said things were going well. As the evening passed, Nate laid down and went to sleep.

As Miss Nancy slept, her dead husband came to her in a dream. He looked a young man at peace. He told Nancy, "Nate would be called home, but not to be sad. He'd be with me."

The next morning, Miss Nancy and Marry Lou woke up about the same time. The two women talked over breakfast. Nancy didn't tell Marry Lou anything about her dream. After all, it didn't say when, and Mr. Brown said things were going well.

That morning in court, Mr. Brown told Nate and the women he had sent another telegram to the ranger station after court yesterday. "No reply has come so far." Mr. Brown called Nancy and Marry Lou to testify. Both told how decent and honorable Nate was and knew he was innocent.

The prosecutor asked both of them, "Did you see the murder?" Both said no, but knew he didn't do it.

Nate was called to testify. He told the same story he told from the beginning. When Mr. Brown finished, the prosecutor, very hostile, called him a "cold-blooded murderer." He said Nate was after the Johnson's money. Nate began to get angry. Mr. Brown objected. The judge ruled the prosecutor was doing fine in his treatment of Nate. Mr. Brown asked for a few moments to calm his client. The judge said no and told Mr. Brown to sit down.

Nate stood up, "Mr. Brown, why are they..." Before he could finish his question, the judge ordered the sheriff to restrain Nate. The judge told Mr. Brown to control his client or he'd be shackled.

"Judge, if I could have a few moments, I am sure I could calm my client."

"You best do that. You have 15 minutes," said the judge, with an anger heard in his voice.

Mr. Brown went to Nate, put his arms around his shoulder and calmed him down. He told Nate, "You need to stay seated on the stand. If you get aggressive, it looks bad."

"I am not a cold-blooded killer," said Nate, confused and angry.

"We know that Nate. It is the prosecutor's job to make you look guilty. When you get aggressive, you help them win. Now you are going to sit back down on the stand and stay calm. He is ok now, sheriff."

The sheriff let Nate go back to the stand. "Did you kill the Johnson's?" snapped the prosecutor.

"The bible says thou shall not kill," stated Nate.

The prosecutor asked the judge to order Nate to answer the question. He did.

"I follow the bible's teachings," said Nate.

"Is that a yes or no?" asked the judge, losing patience.

"It is a no, sir," replied Nate.

Nate was excused. Mr. Brown called Doc James to the stand. He spoke of Nates' character and honesty, how long he knew Nate, how he always gave pay to his mother and how he always spoke fondly of the Johnson's.

The prosecutor asked Doc James, "Did you see the murder?"

"No," replied the doctor.

"So you don't know if Nate killed the Johnson's?" stated the prosecutor.

"I know he didn't because I have known Nate and his family since he was a little boy."

The doctor was excused. Mr. Brown asked for a continuance until after dark that day to present new evidence and reconvene at the scene of the murder. The judge agreed.

After the prosecutor agreed, Mr. Brown explained what he was going to do to Nate and the others away from the rest of the people in the court.

Nate, his mother and Marry Lou during the recess were allowed to visit with a guard present. The hour visit went fast. That night everybody met in front of the Johnson's store. Mr. Brown asked the court bailiff to enter the store by the back door without the benefit of a lantern. A few moments later, the judge, prosecutor, and jury entered the front door with a lantern. They saw the bailiff laying on top of sacks of flour and the bailiff was covered in flour. Mr. Brown pointed out to all those there this proves Nate could be covered with blood from the Johnsons' bodies without killing them. The defense rested. That night, Nate dreamt his mother stood by a grave, crying.

In court the next day, Nate told his mother about his dream. She told Nate heaven watches over us all as she smiled and hugged him. She didn't talk about the dream she had. She just held him tight. "They are going to say I did it," Nate said as she hugged his mother.

"Heaven watches over us all. Get your strength from heaven," his mother said.

After closing arguments, the judge sent the jury to deliberate. Nate sat in the jail and the guard looked at him and smiled. "It's ok." Nate and Nancy asked each other where Marry Lou might be. Neither had seen Marry Lou since last night. Nate asked Mr. Brown if he had seen or heard from Marry Lou.

"I saw her having dinner with a friend," said Mr. Brown. He didn't tell Nate it was a man and they were holding hands. When Marry Lou saw him, she stopped holding his hand and smiling. They hardly finished their dinner and left together.

Mr. Brown stood up and asked if he could have a recess so they could look at some new evidence for the defense. He felt he may have found the murderer. The judge agreed.

Mr. Brown told the sheriff what he saw. The sheriff wired the sheriff in Marry Lou's hometown asking him to hold Marry Lou and her friend till told different, should the two show up there. Nate and Miss Nancy asked Mr. Brown why he did that.

"Be patient," he replied. The prosecutor, Mr. Brown, and the judge met in chambers. After the meeting, the judge ordered the jury to hold up on a verdict for 5 days. He also released Nate on bail. He had to stay in town.

The sheriff sent a deputy to look for Marry Lou and the young man. The deputy rode for a day before he found a young man's body that had been stabbed many times. He was clutching a piece of yellow cloth torn from an article of clothing. The deputy brought the body back to town, being careful not to lose the piece of cloth.

On the deputy's return, he was sent to Marry Lou's town to look for her. On the way he stopped at a ranch house. The owner told him he found a young woman on his range unconscious. She had been snake-bit. He took her to his house. She was in the bedroom. He showed the deputy the woman. She was wearing a yellow dress. It was on the chair. The deputy examined it. The tear on the dress matched the cloth from the young man's hand. The two men sat at the table and talked as the deputy took notes.

The next morning the woman woke up. She asked where she was. The rancher told her she had been bit by a snake and had brought her to his ranch to recover.

"Where is my dress?" she asked.

"On the chair," replied the rancher. "What's your name?"

"Marry Lou. My horse ran away. I had to walk."

The sheriff's deputy entered the room. "Her name is Marry Lou," the rancher told him.

"Can she travel?"

"I don't know why not," said the rancher.

"Why is there a hole in your dress?" the deputy asked Marry Lou.

"I don't know," replied Marry Lou.

The deputy made arrangements with the rancher to rent one of his wagons to take her back to the county seat. It was a little over a day away. The deputy put handcuffs on Marry Lou and chained her to the wagon. On the way, Marry Lou cussed the deputy. She also tried to lure him with her feminist whiles.

"Why did you kill them?" asked the deputy.

"They were going to leave half the store and money to Nate," she replied. "I didn't. The man on the range did for $500. After we got the money, we were going to Mexico, but he tried to cheat me, so I killed him. Try to prove it," she said, defiantly. The deputy did not respond.

The next morning, the two arrived at the county seat. The deputy checked Marry Lou into the jail. The sheriff sent a message to the judge that Marry Lou was being held in jail. He also sent the same message to the prosecutor and Mr. Brown, Nate, and Miss Nancy. The prosecutor and Mr. Brown went to the jail to interview Marry Lou. After the two men talked to the deputy first, they began their interview with Marry Lou. She denied everything she said to the deputy. She did not know how her dress got blood on it or had a tear in it.

After the interview, the D.A. and Mr. Brown went to see the judge. Nate and Nancy came to see Marry Lou. She told the deputy she did not want to see or talk to them. They asked the deputy what was going on. He told them they'd have to talk to him. Both Nate and Nancy were confused, a little angry and distraught.

As Nate and Nancy walked to the diner, they met Mr. Brown. The three sat at the table talking while they ate. Nancy said, "It's hard to believe."

"It's a lie," Nate got upset. "She loves me and I love her." Mr. Brown tried to calm Nate down. It wasn't working. Mr. Brown told Nate to come outside with him. They sat on a bench while Mr. Brown explained the situation to Nate. Nate was saddened. "Why would she do that, Mr. Brown?"

"I don't know Nate. Greed, I guess. The judge has scheduled a court hearing for you tomorrow morning. At that time, charges against you will be dropped."

"I want to see her," demanded Nate. Still a little upset, the two men joined Nancy in the diner and finished their meal. Nate and Nancy were both happy that Nate was exonerated and sad at Marry Lou's behavior. The rest of that day and night went very slow for Nate. He cried in his bed that night, his heart broken. During the night, he heard gunfire. He went outside to see what was happening. He saw Marry Lou riding a horse. She pointed a gun at Nate and shot him. Nancy came outside and saw Nate lying on the sidewalk, bleeding bad. He was dead. Nancy held her son in her arms crying. Both her and Nates' dreams had come true.

Some

A short essay sure to make the reader contemplate the dark nature of man.

Some

Each day brings they whom seek relief. The young, the old, every woman and child. Starting as early as sunrise. Depending on the season, some don't survive the long night. Some perish during the journey. Some perish when caught up in the unrest of those whom seek relief. Some perish whom use violence to take away another's relief. All want the relief. All seek the relief.

Why is this relief so hard to come by? Why do some try to keep others from getting relief? Why are they who come for relief willing to fight and die for it? Is it right that the very young, very old, and those too weak may perish, never getting their relief? You might say some already have received their relief and don't recognize it as such or know what it is. Do you seek your relief? Have you found it? Do you know it when it comes? Do you have the relief you seek? Most don't.

A Man's Thoughts

Take a seat with a group of soldiers as they contemplate the state of our changing world.

A Man's Thoughts

Soldiers in the United States military, each a different race, sat at a table at military camp in a combat zone. A television in the recreation hall was talking about social discord in America. The soldiers looked at each other. After a short time, one of them spoke.

"I have not experienced it."

"I have," said another.

"How so?" asked another.

"I was denied a job because of the affirmative action policies in the 1970's."

"I was refused service in a restaurant in Washington, D.C. being a man of color, and told to leave. It was 1990.

"I also was refused service in South Bend, Indiana in 1988. The waitress stated we don't serve whites here."

Another woman said her parents were held in a detention camp during WWII. They were eventually financially compensated.

One told how his father was denied medical care because of his age.

The man that developed and perfected blood typing was refused treatment at a hospital in America because of his skin color. He died from loss of blood.

6 million Jews were murdered in Europe by Hitler's government, during WWII. In the Middle East, Muslim terrorists have beheaded, burned alive, buried alive and sold into slavery

thousands of men, women, children and babies because they are Christian, and refused to devote themselves to their god.

I ask myself as well as, maybe others should ask themselves, why does mankind tolerate such cruel and disgusting behavior from their fellow humans? I have to wonder what god might do or say about it all if on earth today. Abraham Lincoln said it best. "A house divided cannot stand. The whole world is a big house, and it's about to fall."

She

Delve into the world of the

supernatural through this beautiful tale

of hope.

She

She is a woman of small stature with small features. She is of dark complexion with big, dark eyes. She wears a long, flowing, all-white beautiful embroidered and beaded lace dress with sleeves that covered her arms down to her hands. A laced black scarf covered all of her hair. What you can see of her shoes appear to be all leather. Her hat is all white, round with a wide brim and decorated in the front with a heart-shaped decoration made of precious stones and embroidered with silver lines. The back has a small round design made of precious stones and red and silver lines. She wears a long necklace of red, black, and yellow cloth sporting a jeweled ambulette.

She walks with graceful, deliberate motion. She has a non-emotional, but non-threatening look on her face. In her company are two small children with black hair. They are about four or five years old. Caring for the children is an older woman wearing modest clothing, with non-distinguishing features.

The woman in white walked through the waiting room and down all of the hallways. She spoke not. There were a lot of people waiting to be treated. There was a young mother, her daughter sat in a wheelchair, her body deformed and unable to speak. A young soldier blinded in combat sat next to his wife, holding her infant child in her arms. There were some older people, some in wheelchairs, some using walkers, some using oxygen. Once more, the woman in white walked through the waiting room and stood there.

The young girl with the deformed body spoke. "Mama, I'm hungry. Can we go home and eat?" The girls' mother did not respond. The young girl touched her mother on the shoulder and spoke again. "Mama, I'm hungry."

The mother looked up. For the first time in 12 years of her daughter's life, she heard her daughter speak and she was standing tall and straight. The mother began to weep with joy and stood up and hugged her child, still weeping.

"Mama, why do you weep?" the child asked.

At the same time, the blind soldier spoke to his child. "You look so pretty in your pink pj."

His wife looked at him. "How did you know her pj was pink?"

"I can see them," he replied. "I can see. I can see."

"What am I wearing?" she asked him.

"A blue t-shirt, white shorts, and a baseball cap."

She began to weep for joy. "It's a miracle!" she exclaimed.

The old people in the wheelchairs could now walk. All of the people's afflictions were no more. They all knelt and began to pray. The woman in white walked away, saying nothing.

After a while, the doctor came into the waiting room, demanding to know what was going on. There was no response from the people. The doctor said, "you cannot pray here. It is against policy." The doctor fell to the floor, unable to move. The rest of the medical staff fell to their knees, and began to pray. The doctor began to pray. Once again, he was able to move. He rose to his feet and sent for the chaplain.

When the chaplain arrived, the doctor told him what happened. The chaplain said a prayer. He asked the people about their experiences. As it turned out, all the sick in the clinic that day were healed. They all spoke of the woman in white. Was it the second coming? Had the clinic become a shrine?

Word of what happened went all the way to the top of the chain of command. Leaders from the religious community came from all over the world seeking understanding of what happened that day. The news media were demanding access to the clinic. Politicians came for the photo ops at the clinic.

For some reason, beyond their understanding, the politicians fell ill upon entering the clinic. There was talk of shutting it down for fear it might be contaminated. The thing was, only those seeking notoriety fell ill. Those seeking to heal or pray didn't fall ill. In some way, names and contact information of the people at the clinic that day was leaked to the media.

The media offered large amounts of money to anyone willing to go public with their story. Only one accepted the offer. After their story was released, they went on a talk show. While on the show, the host as well as the guest were struck down and died. This caused even more media frenzy. People all over the world experienced either fear or feeling of warmth and comfort from their faith. Some religious leaders declared the end of the world was coming. Others spoke of loving your fellow man and worshipping god and forgiveness. Most world leaders sought peace for their nations. Others saw the events as an opportunity to further their political gains.

Once again, mankind had missed their chance to achieve peace in the world, but instead sought personal gain. Was the woman in white the second coming, or evil come to tempt mankind? I don't know, what do you think?

Mr. Rich

A story of kindness, compassion, and love

for humanity that shows the joys of

helping others.

Mr. Rich

He was an older man. One could see he had a hard life. He seemed to know everybody, always smiling and pleasant, although not always for the same reason. From time to time, some whispered in his ear. Others waved and yelled across the room and waved always with a smile. It seemed the women openly showed him affection. They'd greet him with hugs and kisses on his face. It wasn't just the old or young. They all did. As to whether he was a man of means or a pauper, no one seemed to know. They knew he was always helping one person or another, buying them a sandwich, handing them a couple dollars or just giving them a ride somewhere. They called him Mr. Rich. It was a term of endearment and respect.

He dressed like that of a man that enjoyed being comfortable. He didn't seem to be impressed by those in expensive clothing. By the same token, those in rags didn't tug on his heart strings either. If one became a nuisance, they only did it once.

The one called Jay, a bright young man, worked the streets. He used and sold weed. He had reached the tender age of 19, unprepared for life, in any sense of the word. After a few interactions with Jay, of encouraging him to go to a trade school, each time Jay told Mr. Rich he entered into a welder apprenticeship program. He asked him if he was going to stay with it.

Jay said, "yes, sir."

"You best understand," stated Mr. Rich.

"Yes, sir!" repeated Jay. To date, Jay works as a welder apprentice at the ship yards. He no longer works the streets.

Susan, a young mother of three, was being beaten and sexually abused by her ex-boyfriend after a night of heavy drinking. Calling the police only kept him locked up for a day. His family would bail him out. The day came when Mr. Rich received a call from Susan.

"Don't anger him. Be there soon," he ordered.

Upon entering the apartment, Susan was in tears, begging Ron to not kill her baby, promising anything and everything.

Mr. Rich held her by the arm. "You need to calm down and be quiet now!" he said firmly. "Are you hurt at all?"

"No, but my baby!" she said upset. "He is in the bedroom."

Mr. Rich courteously approached the bedroom. Appearing in the room, he saw Ron, Susan's ex, sitting on a rocking chair, holding a gun and the baby. The baby was asleep and appeared to be unharmed. Walking into the room like he owned it, speaking calm, but firm, Mr. Rich said, "Ron, this cannot be exactly good for you. What troubles you, that you see the need to hold a child hostage?"

"She wants to dump me, the bitch," Ron said, with an attitude.

"And holding this child hostage helps your situation how?" replied Mr. Rich. "Gently hand me the baby and lay the gun down on the floor."

Ron did as he was told. Mr. Rich called Susan to come get the child.

The child being out of danger and united with its mother, "Ron, would you like to walk out of here like nothing happened today?"

"It is too late. I'm screwed," said Ron.

"Ron, you leave the gun where it lies and leave peaceful-like and we all good. No police, no nothing, ok, and bother Susan no more, agree?"

"Yes, sir!" answered Ron.

"Now be gone with yourself," ordered Mr. Rich. With that, Ron left and never bothered Susan again.

Mr. Rich walked down the sidewalk on a cold, starry night. When he came upon a man, a rather large man, being abusive to a much smaller woman, he put his hands in his coat pockets, and walked up to the couple. "Ma'am, is this something you wish to continue?"

She started to answer, but before she could go on, the man told her, "Shut up! She ain't nobody. You best get before I kick your ass. You either crazy or your..." After a slight pause, he let go of the woman. "You got a gun in your pocket, don't you?"

"Maybe yes. Maybe no," replied Mr. Rich. "How bad you want to know?"

The man told the woman, "come on," as he grabbed her arm.

"I ain't going with you. Do I have to go with him?" she asked Mr. Rich,

"Not if you don't want to," stated Mr. Rich. "Young man, I suggest you walk away and leave the lady here." Mr. Rich went on, as the man walked away leaving the woman behind.

"You motherfucker best be carrying that gun the next time we meet," as he disappeared down the street.

The woman asked Mr. Rich if he would have shot the abusive man.

"Not likely. I don't have a gun."

The events in this story actually happened. Names and places were changed to protect peoples' privacy.

Green River

Dive into the world of crime and mobster as willy and his friends cruise the country!

Green River

The big black car drove down the dirt road at a high speed. The four occupants of the car, three women and the driver, a large, not-so-bright, but very strong man, wanted to put distance between them and the town where they just robbed a syndicate bank. The year is 1933. Due to the Great Depression and the Volstead act making alcohol illegal, crime was rampant, everything from murder to bootlegging. A new breed of criminal was born. People went from poverty to wealthy because of the prohibition. Men and women who couldn't find honest work, worked for gangsters, driving trucks, working in speakeasies, and dime-a-dance clubs. They also made booze in their homes. Getting back to the big black car, Willy, the driver, and his three female friends, Dee, Lilly, and Carmen, had to melt into the population, and quickly. If the mob caught up with them, they would be killed. All four of them carried .45 pistols and Willie had a tommy gun.

"Stop!" Dee told Willy.

"What's wrong?" asked Willy. The sign said 'Green River, population 65.'

"This is a good place to disappear," stated Dee. "Pull over. Let's put the guns in the boot. As far as people hear, we are a vaudeville act and going to our next job. Don't nobody do nothing to draw attention to us."

Now, Green River is a scenic, quiet valley by a flowing river. The sign under the town name advertised a lodging two miles down the road. The lodge was quaint and rustic looking, on a wooden lot. The cabins cost $5 a day, with meals included. Dee and Lilly went into the rental office and rented two cabins. They were told there would be a $1.50 a day extra for the two-extra people. The clerk told them they were just in time for lunch. The clerk was a woman about 40-years-old. She told Dee and Lilly her and her father owned the lodge.

"We would like a cabin in the back," stated Dee.

"No problem," said the clerk.

Willy parked the car in the back and joined the ladies in the dining room. The owner brought four plates of food to the table. Willy asked her if she had any liquor.

"We have beer," she replied.

"Please bring four glasses," said Lil.

"Where's the town?" asked Dee.

"It ain't much of a town. We have a small general store and a pump gas station. Our barber is also our dentist. We had a doctor, but he died. His wife treats minor injuries and illness. There is a diner in town as well. The food here is better. So is the liquor. Men outnumber women four to one. Most young women leave here first chance they get. Can't say I blame them. Most men here are selfish drunks. Can I get you another beer?" the owner asked.

"Yes," said Willy. "And a bucket to take back to the cabin."

When the owner brought the beer to the table, Carmen asked if they sold cigarettes. "Yes, ma'am," the owner replied. "10 cents a pack."

"We will take four packs. Do you get a lot of strangers in town," asked Lil.

"Not often," answered the owner. "You folks are the first strangers in months. Sometimes we get liquor runners come through town. They make a delivery and move on. Sometimes they stop at the yellow house at the edge of town," as she smiled.

"What's there?" asked Willy.

"They provide entertainment for the men folks in town," replied the owner.

"What's your name?" asked Willy, of the owner.

"I'm Sally. What's your name?" she answered.

Dee hit Willy on the knee and shook her head. "His name is Charlie." Willy understood. No real names. Carmen was sweet on Willy. So was Lil and Dee. Now, Willy was a horndog. He enjoyed all three of the women's affections as often as possible. Willy always figured there was room for one more. The four went to their cabins, taking their bucket of beer.

The women told Willy he need not chase Sally. They'd take care of his needs, and did. The ladies impressed upon Willy, strangers could bring trouble upon them. Willy agreed, although in his mind, he was attracted to Sally. It didn't take long to drink the beer. Willy said, "I'll get more."

"Oh no, you won't," said Dee. "You might get sidetracked. I'll go." And she did.

Dee returned and told the others the lodge had gambling in the back room. Now, Lil and Carmen expressed concern that gambling would bring mob members to the lodge, bringing a problem for them. They discussed it for some time. They finally agreed they would play it by ear and check out the back room. If they saw anybody that looked like trouble, they would deal with it then. They did, however, carry their .45's.

When the four entered the back room, Willy noticed Sally was wearing a low-cut dress and looking good, unlike the way she looked when they first arrived. "It would appear Sally is not the chick we thought she was," said Carmen. There were 15 or 20 people in the room. Most in overalls. There were four women in the room, not counting Lil, Dee, or Carmen.

Sally walked up to Willy and touched his shoulder. "Glad you came," said Sally, with a big smile on her face. Willy returned her greeting, also with a big smile.

"Walk with me to the bar," said Carmen. "You got to leave that woman alone. You are going to cause all kinds of problems for us all.

"I can't ever talk to her?" asked Willy.

"Yes, you can," replied Carmen. "But that's all. You see Willy, Lil, Dee, and me are thinking, maybe we relieve them of the burden of all that cash they got. We need you to make her a non-problem."

"I don't understand," replied Willy.

"Take her to the cabin and put her in an endless sleep."

"I don't understand," Willy said again.

"Kill her and don't use your gun."

"Can I have a little fun first?" asked Willy.

"I suppose so, but don't be all day about it. When you are done, bring the car around to the front. Come back to the back room and bring the tommy gun and come in firing and, Willy remember, don't shoot me, Dee, or Lil."

"I know that," stated Willy, a little angry.

As Willy worked to entice Sally to go with him, Dee, Lil, and Carmen surveyed the back room for any problems. There was lots of cash at the gaming tables. A short time passed, when ten women entered the room all looking like entertainment specialists.

As Sally pleasured Willy, the music on the radio was interrupted. "On this December, 1933, prohibition has been repealed by the U.S. legislators."

For a short moment after being pleasured, Willy told Sally, "thanks, it was fun," while crushing her larynx with his large, strong hands. When sure Sally had passed, he got dressed and got the tommy gun out of the car boot. He set the cabin on fire.

When entering the back room, Willy began firing. At the same time, Dee and Carmen did the same. Some escaped death by running through the exit by the hotel lobby. To their dismay, Lil shot anyone coming through the door. After robbing the dead and the gaming tables, the four left after setting the building on fire.

"Is Sally dead?" asked Lil, of Willy.

"Yes," he replied. As the big black car went down the dirt road, the occupants counted their ill-gotten booty. They had no way of knowing their deed would bring them hell on earth.

After driving, for what seems for hours, they came to a small town with a pump gas station general store. It looked really familiar. On entering the store, Carmen grabbed Willy's hand, digging her nails into his hand.

"What's wrong with you?" asked Willy.

"Look at the store clerk. Let's get out of here, now," said Dee, fear in her voice.

"Ask if they sell beer," said Lil.

The store clerk turned and faced the four of them.

"It can't be," declared Willy.

Sally stood before them, her skin charred from fire. "Welcome back, lover."

"You're...you're...a...a," Willy finally able to finish his sentence. "Dead."

"Come honey, make love to me. Don't I please you anymore?" the hideous sally ordered, as she reached out to pull Willy to her. Willy drew his gun and emptied it into Sally. "Come on lover, that's no way to treat a lady." Willy saw his three companions laying on the floor with bullet holes in their bodies. Willy felt a hand grab his arm. It was Sally. Willy began to scream. He couldn't pull his arm loose, still screaming. "You my man now honey, til the end of time." Willy fell to the floor dead of a heart attack. Sally knelt down and kissed Willy on the lips. "You my man now."

Dreadlocks

A Story of mystery, murder, and family sure to keep its reader on the edge of there seat.

Dreadlocks

His dreadlocks came halfway down his back. Being tall and young, with his heavy thick black beard, and big smile, I am guessing makes him a catch for many young women. Speaking of young women, a blonde, maybe mid 20's, 5'5'' tall, fair complexion, her lipstick being red, with her perfect figure, and long flowing hair also a catch for men of any age. She could be a professional model or actress. There was another individual in the restaurant who was also tall and really thin, and not too clean. As he gave his order to the cashier, Dreadlocks walked up to the cashier and demanded all the money or someone will bleed.

The cashier, a high school girl, started to scream and cry. The blonde approached the cashier. "Pull yourself together, do like he tells you and you will be ok."

About that time, the manager took over the cashier's place. "We will do anything you say. Just don't hurt anyone."

Dreadlocks was getting impatient. "Hurry up or a lot of people are going to bleed. If the police come before I'm gone, everybody dies."

The manager, while messing her pants, did as Dreadlocks ordered.

Dreadlocks grabbed the blonde by the hair. "You come with me. If anybody tries to stop me, the bitch dies, dig?" He dragged her to his car, while she was screaming all the way. "Drive," he ordered the blonde. She did, shortly after Dreadlocks left the robbery scene.

The police came. After interviewing everybody in the restaurant, the high school girl and the manager stated they need a change of clothes and were allowed to leave. The tall, thin, not so clean man was detained by the police, at which he protested loud and vulgar-like. The police cuffed him and took him in.

After hours of interrogation, they determined he was not involved in the robbery. A description of Dreadlocks and the blonde went out to the public as no one saw the car he left in.

As Dreadlocks sped away from the restaurant, both him and the blonde were ecstatic. They pulled off the perfect crime. "Dreadlock, no one knows what you really look like, except me," stated Blondie. "All I got to do is show up in a day or two looking raped and abused."

"We are going to take care of that right now, pull over here," Dreadlock ordered. She did. Both got out of the car, happy and smiling. Dreadlock pointed his gun at Blondie and shot her, killing her. "Now it is the perfect crime. Nobody knows what I look like."

For days, the gruesome crime was all over the news. The public demanded justice for Blondie. Some donated money to her husband to pay for her funeral. A memorial of flowers was started where she was murdered.

As Cindy and her mother ate breakfast, they talked about the rent being past due and how they might pay it. "I made some good tips the last two days. I have the rent. I'll pay the landlord today." She handed her mother $20 in singles. Cindy kissed her mom as she left for work.

After mom left, Cindy got dressed and counted her cash on hand. She'd have to work a second job again soon. Cindy sat drinking her coffee, studying Veaka. Veaka is young and really cute, with a really nice figure, and a taste for cocaine. Over a period of days, Cindy has established a repertoire with Veaka. Her expensive habit made her the perfect partner in crime. Not to mention, Cindy, being a short, not so attractive woman, resented women like Veaka. She and Cindy sat and drank coffee. While doing so, Cindy studied Veaka's every mannerism. She was always careful to never reveal anything that might give her true ideas too soon. She was almost sure Veaka was the one. She would let mom know her decision soon.

After talking to mom, it was decided Veaka wouldn't do. "Junky can't be trusted. They are too chatty." Mom did suggest burning her for a quick grand, if done right. Cindy told Veaka she knew where she could get $2000 worth of cocaine for $1500. If she tells anybody where she is getting it, the deal is off. Now, Cindy knew it might take a little time. She knew Veaka didn't have $1500, but knew other junkies that would come across with what money Veaka didn't have. After all, cocaine is a bitch of a master. She wants her due at any cost.

Mom called Decon. Now, Decon is a cold, callous, vulgar person who worships the dollar. He is terminally ill with nothing to lose. He would furnish a small amount of cocaine to let the mark see the product, if she had the $1500 on her. Decon had Veaka meet him at a nearby gas station.

After being sure she was alone and not being followed, they went to a house. They went into a room. Veaka gave Decon $1500. Decon made a phone call. Shortly after, Tiny, a large, unpleasant women weighing nearly 400 pounds, came in the room. "You got the $1500?

"Yes," answered Decon. "You didn't exaggerate. Here's your $1000."

"What's going on? Where is my cocaine?" Veaka demanded. The woman hit her so hard she knocked her out of her chair.

"Congratulations, you're hired. Now get your ass off the floor. I'll let you know when you can talk. Until then, keep your mouth shut." With that the large woman left with Veaka. "Catch you next time, Decon. You get cocaine when I say, if and when you've worked for it."

"Tell mom, I'll be over for dinner Sunday, as usual."

"See you then," answered Decon. Mom passed the word to the family Sunday dinner will be at papa's, for everybody should be there.

"Do you have something for me, Decon?" mom asked. Decon handed mom an envelope full of money. "How about the other thing, Cindy?" asked mom. "Still screening for a good candidate?"

She replied, "I have three. I am looking at all young, really attractive, shallow, not too bright, that want to rebel against their parents."

"Maybe we use all three the same day. Timed right, it should work," said mom. "We check it out."

"When?" asked Cindy.

"After lunch," replied mom. "We do one at a time, an hour apart.

Mom and Cindy observed the three young girls, listening to their conversations. They talked about pooling their money and going to California, maybe going in the movies. One of the girls said, "females make thousands a day in porn movies."

The other two agreed. "We do it anyway. Why not get paid for it?"

"You know they sound like truck drivers with their constant cussing," pointed out mom. "It's just terrible. They're perfect. We use them. Just make sure they sober and watch their mouths, after all, they have to appear to be polite young ladies, you know, victims."

"Dreadlocks is in Miami for the next couple days. We set it for a week from today," suggested Cindy.

"Sounds good," replied mom. "Maybe this time we let them live. Tiny has a large order to fill. We will have to see how troublesome they are afterwards. We will leave it up to Dreadlocks as each one goes down."

After a relaxing barbeque at papa's on Sunday, mom and papa had a short meeting while sipping sherry. After meeting with Tiny, Dreadlocks, Cindy and Decon, it was agreed that three in one day was doable, as long as Decon was at a place waiting, with Tiny to take the girls off Dreadlocks hands after each job. If any of the girls became too much of an inconvenience they'd be done away with. Also, there would be two hours between each job, giving Tiny and Decon time to deal with each previous girl.

Cindy went to work recruiting the girls, never telling them more than they needed, just dangling money in front of each of them which they immediately jumped at. It was all set. Tomorrow was the day.

That morning, two cars were stolen and two more in case they were needed. Very early that morning, mom and papa talked.

"Don't do the heist, not enough money in it. Just snatch the girls. Tiny, you be there to receive them. Dreadlocks and Decon will snatch them. Get them all at one time. Don't frighten them. They got to think money. Tell them they're going to make $1000 a day each for four days work in a movie."

The word went out. The new plan began. All three did the job. Mom sat on papa's boat drinking moonshine cocktails. Cindy and Tiny were ready for the girls. The whole thing took less than an hour.

A delivery man stood on the dock. "Pizza delivery! Is this the Sweet T?". Mom took the pizza, tipped the boy, sat with papa and ate pizza, congratulating each other on a good business day.

They couldn't have expected the call. "Hello," answered mom.

"They are raiding Tiny's place. What should we do?" the voice spoke.

"Call Nails. After he posts bail for those arrested, have Decon go by the jail where they exit. Decon should inform them of their retirement benefits. Make sure Tiny and the other arrested completely understand them. Dreadlock, you drive the car. See to it all those arrested are retired on the spot, Nails is not to retire yet."

Upon exiting the jail, Tiny and Cindy were met by a hail of bullets. Both lay dead in front of the jail in a pool of their own blood. As Dreadlocks raced away from the jail, Decon said he'd been shot. Blood gushed from his belly. He was slipping into unconsciousness. Dreadlocks stopped at a mall parking lot where he abandoned the car with Decons' body still in it. Dreadlocks set the car ablaze.

That night on the news, they told of the gangland style murder, of the two sex trade defendants, a policeman also lay dead on the sidewalk. The public was outraged. Dreadlocks checked into a motel and called mom as directed. Mom told Dreadlocks a delivery would be made to his room. Now Dreadlocks thought this unusual, but he dismissed it. After all, nobody knew what he really looked like. He figured they were sending get away money.

There was a knock on the door. He casually opened the door. Standing there was a beautiful, young woman. She was dressed to entice and entertain. "I am Janine. Mom sent me to take care of your needs." Again, Dreadlocks saw no need for concern.

Now, Dreadlocks, being a lesbian, was beside herself with excitement over Janine. After taking care of the Dreadlocks needs, Janine lay on the bed waiting for Dreadlocks to come out of the bathroom. After waiting several moments, Janine knocked on the bathroom door. "Come in," Dreadlocks said. Janine opened the door holding a gun in her hand. Dreadlocks sat on the toilet, also holding a gun. Janine fired first. Dreadlocks died, sitting on the toilet. Janine got dressed and put her gun away. She set about planting the fire bomb. After setting the timer, Janine walked to the door. She was planning her next mark in her thoughts.

"What the 'F', why won't this door open?" she said with anger. She played with the locks to no avail. "Damn it. Open, you piece of shit. Damn door." She'd have to call the front desk and quick. This wasn't part of her original plan. The timer and bomb came to mind. Janine got Dreadlocks' and her own gun and fired both at the picture window. It is Janine's back luck. The window is made of plexiglass. Plexiglass doesn't shatter. She then fired the guns at the door lock. The door didn't open. As Janine looked at the door, she said out loud, "son of a bitch. I should have known. Papa doesn't allow any loose ends!" Boom, bang!!!-

Homeless

The heartbreaking story of Helen an innocent young girl thrown into world with no guidance or hope and left to fend for herself.

Homeless

Grandpa Boyd was a rich farmer, who owned a large farm in Ohio. Farmer Boyd had an attractive daughter, Helen, who was full of energy and spirit. She was happy and always curious about what was going on around her and life in general.

Helen was sixteen-years-old and loved living on her father's farm. Each day she looked forward to helping on the farm and taking care of the animals and collecting the eggs in the hen house.

After the morning chores, Helen and her mom and dad would sit down to a large breakfast of eggs and ham or bacon, fresh fried potatoes, milk and fruit, and all the products on the farm.

After breakfast, Helen would shower, get dressed and go to school. Helen was a good student who enjoyed school and always made good grades.

While Helen was in school, grandpa Boyd and his two Mexican-immigrant farm hands did the daily chores on the farm. Grandpa's farm hands were father and son, Clyde, who was in his thirties.

When Helen came home from school, she liked spending time with Clyde. As time went by, Clyde and Helen became romantically involved.

The day came when Helen started to have symptoms of being pregnant. Helen went to mom about it. Mom took Helen to the doctor. The doctor confirmed she was pregnant. Helen cried. Mom asked Helen who the father was and told her they would have to tell dad. Helen knew grandpa Boyd would be angry.

"Clyde is the father," Helen told mom.

"The farm hand?" asked mom.

"Yes," said Helen.

"Your father will definitely be angry," said mom.

When Helen and her mother got home, grandpa asked mom what was wrong with Helen. Mom told Helen to get Clyde and bring him to the house. "Have him wait on the porch," mom said.

"What is going on?" asked grandpa.

"I need you to stay calm. Helen is pregnant and Clyde is the father. I sent Helen to get Clyde." As Helen and Clyde approached the house, they could hear grandpa yelling, "I will kill that son of a bitch. I will not have a bastard in my home."

Helen and Clyde looked at each other. "No way I am going in there," said Clyde.

"You're not going to run out on me, are you?" asked Helen.

"You can come with me if you want, but I'm not staying here." Helen took Clyde's hand. The two of them turned around and quickly walked away from the house. They went to see Clyde's father.

As they approached the house, they saw Clyde's father siting on the porch. Clyde started talking to his father in Spanish. Clyde's father went into the house for a few moments. He came back out and handed Clyde some money and keys and hugged Clyde.

"What is going on?" asked Helen.

"Father gave me the keys to the truck and five hundred dollars and suggests we leave as soon as possible." Helen and Clyde got into the truck. As they drove away, they could see grandpa walking towards the truck. Helen knew she would never see her mom and dad again.

As Helen and Clyde went down the road saying little for what seemed like forever, Clyde said, "We need gas. I am hungry, how about you?"

"Me too," said Helen.

They pulled into the restaurant parking lot and went inside. That sat at a table. The restaurant was a typical truck stop with gas pumps and a greyhound bus stop. "I need some coffee," said Clyde. "What do you want, Helen?"

"Hot chocolate sounds good. Where are we going?"

The waitress came to the table. "What would you like to order? We have a meatloaf dinner for a special today. Here is a menu. What can I get you to drink??

"We will have a cup of coffee and hot chocolate," said Clyde.

"I will get your drinks while you decide what you want to eat."

As Clyde and Helen looked at the menu, Helen said, "I am hungry, tired, and scared."

"My dad had a suggestion. How would you feel about getting an abortion?"

"I think I am going to be sick," said Helen as she got up and quickly went to the bathroom. As she ran to the bathroom, she started crying. As she cried in the bathroom, a woman came in.

"Are you ok? Can I help?" asked the woman. Helen turned and looked at the woman while drying her eyes and told her she was pregnant and the father wanted her to get an abortion.

"I am so scared. I don't know what to do." The woman took Helen in her arms and held her close as she cried.

"You need to pull yourself together. Where is the father?"

Helen backed away from the woman. "He is sitting at a table in the restaurant. I don't want an abortion."

"How long have you been married?" asked the woman.

"I'm not," said Helen.

"Why don't you throw some water on your face and go back to your table and tell the man how you feel. Take this phone number and call if I can help."

Helen put the number in her pocket and went back to the table and sat down.

"I ordered you a hamburger," said Clyde. "Are you ok?"

"No, I'm not. I don't want an abortion. I want to keep our baby." The waitress brought the food and asked if they needed anything else.

"More coffee," said Clyde. The waitress left to get the coffee pot. "I am not ready to be a father. We have no place to live and no income. How are we supposed to raise a baby?" Clyde finished his burger and handed Helen three hundred dollars. "Hang onto this, it is our emergency money. I am going to get gas for the truck and check the oil. You stay here and finish your sandwich. I'll be back as soon as I am done getting gas."

The waitress brought the check and handed it to Helen as she finished her sandwich. Helen looked out the window. She didn't see the truck or Clyde. Helen paid the check and went outside to look for Clyde. She didn't see him. She went back in the restaurant and asked the waitress if she had seen Clyde. The waitress said no.

Helen realized that Clyde had taken off and she was on her own. Helen looked around and saw the woman who had helped her in the bathroom. She was sitting with a man at a table. Helen walked over.

The woman looked up and spoke to Helen. "Hello again. How you getting along?"

"Not so good," said Helen. "He took off and left me," as she started to tear up.

"You know if he is that way you are better off without him. Have a seat. Do you know anybody in the area?"

"No," said Helen.

"How about you call your family. Do you have money for the phone?"

"Yes. He did give me some money before he ran off."

"At least he did that much. You go call your family and we will wait while you do that." Helen went to the phone and called home.

"Hello," the voice said.

"Hello dad. It is Helen."

"Where are you?" asked her father.

"I am at a truck stop about a hundred miles from you. Clyde brought me here, gave me some money and left me here. I need help dad."

"You made your bed, now go and lay in it." With that, her dad hung up the phone. Helen started crying.

She felt a hand on her shoulder and heard a voice say, "I take it things didn't go well." It was the nice woman.

"My father said, you made your bed now go and lay in it," Helen said, crying.

"How about you come with me and my son. We're spending the night at my son's house and then I am going on to Mansfield. Tomorrow when we get there, we will get you some help." Helen followed her back to the table. The two of them sat down. "This is my son, Fred, and my name is Diana. What is your name?"

"My name is Helen and my father has disowned me and I appreciate any help I can get," she said as she dried her tears.

As Fred pulled into his driveway, Helen saw a sign that read 'church service hours'. "Are you a pastor?" asked Helen.

"Yes," said Fred. "When we get settled in for the night, we can talk and make sure you are ok. Ok?"

"Ok."

Diana told Helen she was a registered nurse at a clinic in Mansfield. She went on to say the clinic is free for those who qualify. "I will help you get public assistance and a place to live." They went into the house and settled in for the night.

At daylight, Helen opened her eyes. She felt better about things. There was a knock on the door. Helen got out of bed and opened the door.

"Good morning," said Diana. "I hope you are feeling better this morning."

"Good morning," replied Helen. "I do feel better this morning, but I am hungry."

"Breakfast will be ready shortly. Why don't you take a shower and get dressed? By the time you're done, breakfast should be ready."

Helen could smell the cooking. It smelled good. Helen finished her shower, got dressed and left the bedroom. As she entered the dining room, she saw eggs, sausage, toast, and some juice and coffee. It looked good. Fred was already sitting at the table and Diana came into the room carrying a dish of potatoes.

"Good morning," said Helen.

"Good morning," replied Fred and Diana.

"Have a seat and have breakfast. We will say grace and eat." Diana started passing the food. Helen was hungry. "Eat up. After we eat, would you be willing to help clean up?"

"Glad to," said Helen. Breakfast was delicious. Diana and Helen cleaned up the dishes and the kitchen.

"We need to get going," Diana told Helen. "I'd like to be on the way to Mansfield within the hour so gather your things and we will be on our way, ok?"

"Ok," said Helen. As Helen and Diana went to Mansfield they had a long talk about Helen's situation. Helen was beginning to feel there was hope for her and her baby. After traveling for a couple hours, Helen could see the Mansfield sign saying 'Mansfield 5 miles.' "Mansfield is a big city, with lots of traffic."

"It is about 10 A.M." said Diana. "We will go to my place and I will make a couple of phone calls and see if we can get you a place to live. Then we will go to the public aid office and get you some assistance. How much money do you have?"

"I have two hundred eighty-five dollars," said Helen.

"We should be able to get you an affordable apartment for about $30 to $35 a month. My clinic is near some apartments."

"That would be great," said Helen. Diana pulled up in front of a nice-looking building. "Here we are." The women went to Diana's apartment. "Make yourself comfortable."

Diana sat in a chair and made her phone calls. It was a nice apartment. After a few minutes, they left the apartment and walked back to the car.

"I may have found an apartment," said Diana. "We will go and check it out."

"Great," said Helen.

After a 15-minute ride, they parked in front of a building. Helen could see a drugstore and grocery store close by. The two women went into a building and knocked on a door. An older man opened the door. "Can I help you?" asked the man.

"My name is Diana. May we see the apartment that is available?"

"Give me a minute to get the key," the man said. He showed the two women the apartment. "The rent is $35 a month. It takes two months' rent to move in."

Helen and Diana talked a moment and then Diana told the man, "Helen will take it."

"The lease is month to month, ok?"

"Ok," said Helen. She handed the man $70 and asked for a receipt.

The man took the money and said, "I'll get you a lease and a receipt. Here is the key. I'll be right back."

"After we are done here, next we will stop at public aid," Diana said to Helen. Helen walked around the apartment thinking. She would need sheets, a blanket and food and clothes.

The man came back and handed Helen a receipt and asked her to sign the lease. "It's all yours," said the man. "The rent is due the 1st of each month. If you have any problems, knock on my door. There's a pay phone down the hall."

"Let's take a walk around the neighborhood so you can see what is in the area," Diana said as they walked down the hall to the front door. "There is a diner about a half block from here with a help wanted sign in the window. We can check it out."

As the two women walked, Helen asked Diana if there was a store where she could get some clothes, sheets, and toiletries.

"I've got sheets, a pillow and blanket you can have. As far as toiletries and clothes, there is a store close by and a laundromat."

"Thank you," said Helen.

"Here is the diner. Let's go in and find out about the job." The women sat at the counter. An older woman walked up to them.

"Good morning. Can I help you?" the older woman said.

"Good morning. My name is Helen. Is the job still open?"

The woman looked at Helen a short time. "You look a little young. How old are you?"

"I am 16," answered Helen. "I really need the job and I'll work hard and be here whenever you say."

"This young woman is honest and reliable. She just moved into the neighborhood today. I'm an RN at the clinic just down the block. I'll vouch for her," said Diana.

"I need a dishwasher. You think you can handle it? It pays $30 a week cash plus two free meals a day. It is hard work from 6:00 A.M. to 4 P.M. If you want the job it is yours. There are two 15-minute breaks a day and a 30-minute break for each meal."

"I'll take it," said Helen.

"You start tomorrow. Don't be late."

Helen thanked the woman and said, "I'll be here." She turned to Diana. "I need an alarm clock."

"It's noon. Let's have lunch and then we'll get you the things you need."

A woman came up to them and asked, "Are you eating today?"

"Yes," said Diana. "Can we see a menu, please?"

"Sure thing," said the woman. "What would you like to drink?"

"We will have coffee, please," said Diana.

While the women looked at the menu, the waitress brought their coffee. "Do you see anything you want?"

"The special looks good," said Helen.

"I'll have that too," said Diana. "Thank you."

After lunch, Diana and Helen went to the store and to Diana's house to get sheets, a pillow and a blanket to take them back to Helen's apartment.

"I checked with public aid and they say you have to have a child to get assistance, so after the baby is born, we will go there. I've got to go and get things done. I'll see you soon. If you need anything or have any problems, call me."

"Thank you," said Helen. The two women and hugged and Diana left. Helen got busy making her bed and putting things away. Thanks to Diana, she had everything she needed for a while. She set her alarm for 5:00 A.M. Helen decided to take a walk around the neighborhood and find a store that might have a cheap radio for sale. It was a nice, warm and sunny day. As Helen walked down the street, she awed at all the people on the street and all the traffic. She saw a policeman and walked up to him. "Please, sir. Can you tell me where I might find a store that sells cheap radios?"

"Yes, ma'am. See that big, red and yellow sign? They sell new and used radios," said the policeman as he walked down the street.

"Thank you," said Helen. She started walking toward the sign. Helen saw a number of radios as she entered the store.

An older man approached her. "Good afternoon. Can I help you?"

"Good afternoon," replied Helen. "I am looking for a not-too-expensive radio."

"I have radios from $5 to $50," said the man. He showed Helen his radios. "How much did you want to spend?"

"I don't have a lot of money," said Helen.

"This one is $10 and works and sounds good," said the man.

"Can I hear it work?"

"Sure thing. It has a 30-day warranty." The man turned the radio on. It sounded good and got a lot of stations.

"I'll take it," said Helen. She handed the man $10. "It's kind of big."

"For $2 more, I can deliver it," said the man.

"Ok." She gave him $2 and the address. "When can you deliver it?"

"Today, before 6 P.M." said the man. He gave Helen the receipt.

"Thank you." Helen walked out the door and went home.

When she got home, she made some soup for dinner. There was a knock on the door. Helen answered it. It was the radio delivery man.

"Is this Helen's residence?" asked the delivery man. "I have a radio for you."

"Come in," Helen said. "Can you put it over there, please." Helen watched the man move the radio. He was young, good-looking, and well built. "What's your name?"

"I am Joseph. I live about a block from here."

"I just moved in today. I don't know anybody in town yet. Are you married?"

"No," answered Joe. "Are you?"

"No," said Helen.

"Maybe we can go out sometime," said Joe with a big smile.

"I'd like that," said Helen with a big smile. "I work at the diner down the street from 6 A.M. to 4 P.M.

"Ok," said Joe. "I'll be in touch." As he left, Helen turned the radio to a music station, put on a nightgown, and went to bed. It had been a long and busy day as she was tired.

Helen woke up to her alarm. She felt rested and refreshed. It was the first day of her new job. She looked forward to it. Helen got ready for work and walked to the diner.

The owner showed her to her work station and the things she needed to do her job. "Get yourself some breakfast and start work." Helen did so.

Helen worked hard. The time passed quickly. The owner came and told her she can take her break now. "You've got 15 minutes."

Helen got a drink and sat down at a table. She was tired. The day went fast. She was glad to see 4 P.M. come.

The owner told her she did good and to get supper. "I'll see you tomorrow."

"Thank you," said Helen. She sat eating her dinner. She thought about Joe and when she might see him. When she finished her dinner and took her dishes to the kitchen, she left the diner and went home. She was glad to be off work.

When Helen got home, she took a shower and sat down. She listened to the radio. It was nice to sit and rest. Helen got herself a cup of hot chocolate and continued to listen to the radio.

As the evening passed, there was a knock on the door. It was Joe. Helen's eyes lit up. "Hi Joe, it is good to see you again. Come in."

Joe came in. "I missed you."

"I missed you," said Helen. "Have a seat." As the two sat and talked, they became closer. Helen was getting tired and wanted to go to bed, but she didn't want Joe to leave. "I have to work at 6 A.M. but I don't want you to leave Joe."

"I can stay the night if you want," replied Joe.

"You wouldn't think me easy if I said yes?" said Helen.

"No." They got ready for bed. Helen set her alarm. She was nervous, but happy Joe was staying the night.

The alarm went off. Helen woke up in Joe's arms. It felt good. She hated to get up, but knew she had to go to work. Joe was awake. "Good morning Joe," said Helen.

"Good morning Helen," said Joe.

"Last night was wonderful," said Helen.

"I wouldn't have missed it for the world," said Joe.

"I have to get up and go to work. I'll miss you and get off at 4 P.M. Maybe we can get together after work if you want to."

"I have to work today myself. I get off work at 6 P.M. Maybe we can go to the movies tonight," said Joe.

Helen got ready for work, kissed Joe, and left.

The day went well and fast for Helen. After she ate her dinner, she asked the owner what day she had off. The owner told her Saturday and Sunday.

When Helen got home, she took a shower and called Diana. She told her all about Joe.

Diana said she was happy she had a new friend and asked her if she told Joe she was pregnant. "You have to, you know."

"I know," said Helen. "What if he won't see me anymore. I really like him a lot."

"You owe it to him to be upfront and honest with him. If he cares for you, he will come back. You need to come to the clinic and be seen by a doctor soon."

"Ok," said Helen. "Bye."

That night Helen and Joe went to the movies. They had a good time. Helen knew she had to tell Joe she was pregnant that night and hope he wouldn't dump her.

When they got back to Helen's apartment, Helen turned the radio on. As they sat there, Helen said, "Joe, I need to tell you something. Please let me finish before you say anything."

"Ok," said Joe.

"I'm pregnant. It's not yours. I don't expect you to support the child or give it your name. I really like you. If you don't want to see me anymore, I'll understand."

Joe sat quiet for a short time. "How far along are you?" he asked.

"Two months," said Helen. Joe sat quiet. "You're not angry, are you?"

"How do you feel about staying together. My lease is up soon. What do you think?" asked Joe.

Helen gave Joe a big hug and started to cry. "Yes, yes," she said. "The sooner the better."

"There is no need to cry. Everything will be alright," said Joe and he hugged Helen.

"I think I love you," said Helen.

"I think I love you," said Joe.

They hugged for a long time. "What do we do first?" Helen asked Joe.

"You will have to tell the super I will be moving in," replied Joe.

"It is late. I have to work tomorrow." They went to bed. That night Helen slept in Joe's arms, feeling safe and full of hope for her and her baby's future.

The next day, they went to their jobs both happy and feeling good.

As the time passed, Helen and Joe grew closer together. Helen showing more, it became more difficult to do her job. The owner asked her how far long she was. Helen told her about 7 months. The owner told Helen the cashier was leaving soon. She would have his job and if she needed to rest, then she could take a break.

"Today is Friday. Starting Monday, you are the cashier," said the owner. "Same pay."

"Thank you."

That night, Joe met Helen. As they walked home, Helen told Joe about her job change.

Joe told her he got a raise. They decided to go out to celebrate.

On the way home that night, they talked about getting a car and a new phone with the six hundred dollars they had saved.

The next day, they bought a 1940 Ford with a radio and whitewall tires. It had automatic transmission. It was a beautiful, blue 4-door. They felt proud as they drove down the street. They stopped at the phone company to get a phone and went home.

Six weeks had passed. Being the cashier was much easier than washing dishes. The owner gave Helen a stool to sit on so she wouldn't have to stand so much. That July day in 1947, as Helen was working, her water broke.

She called the waitress nearby. "I need help. My water just broke. Please tell Diana and tell her." Helen gave her the number to call. A few minutes later, Diana came and took her to the hospital.

Helen delivered twin boys, one stillborn. She named the surviving twin, Ron. While she was staying in the hospital, Diana got Helen signed up for public aid. Helen called Joe after the delivery. Joe came to the hospital and stayed by her bedside when not working. Helen felt relieved not being pregnant.

For about 3 months, life was good. Helen took Ron to the clinic for his checkup. While there, she told the doctor she didn't feel so good. The doctor examined her.

"I don't know if this is good news or bad news," said the doctor. "You are pregnant."

"No," said Helen. "Are you serious?"

"I am afraid so."

When she left the doctor exam, she told Diana what the doctor said. "I don't know how Joe is going to react to the news."

"You might start by telling him after the baby is born, you will get more money from public aid," said Diana. "Call me if I can be of help." Helen gave Diana a hug and went home.

For a few months, things were good with Joe and Helen. After that, Joe started drinking, staying up late, and stopped going to work. When Helen would say something to Joe about it, he left the house and stayed out all night. Eventually, he stopped coming home. Helen had to give up the phone. She could no longer pay the bill.

A month later, Helen went to the clinic. She didn't see Diana. She asked the nurse if Diana still worked there. She hadn't heard from her in a while. The nurse told her Diana passed two weeks ago.

Helen was devastated and started crying. Diana was her friend. The nurse told her, "Helen, services were a week ago. Are you going to be ok? Take a seat and get your composure back. Maybe you can see the doctor while you are here."

"Ok," said Helen.

After the doctor examined her and the baby, he gave her the name and phone number of a woman with the salvation army and told her to call her. She could be a big help to her. Helen left the clinic and went home.

Helen sat in the rocking chair Diana gave her and nursed Ron until he fell asleep. She laid Ron in his crib. She went to the kitchen and got lunch for herself.

As she ate her lunch, there was a knock on the door. Helen opened the door. It was Fred, Diana's son. Helen asked him in. They exchanged pleasantries and condolences. Fred explained to Helen, his mother left her a thousand dollars in her will. Fred told Helen, his mother thought of her as the daughter she never had. Helen told Fred, Diana was like a mother to her.

"She talked about you often," said Fred.

"I miss her very much." Fred and Helen talked a while longer. They hugged and said their goodbyes and Fred left.

Helen opened the envelope. There was a thousand dollars cash, a paper with Fred's phone number, and a short note saying 'call me if I can be of help.' Helen put the money and note where it can be safe, turned on the radio, sat back in the rocking chair and took a nap.

After her nap, she changed the baby and went to Wiebolts to buy a baby buggy for two and then went to dinner where she used to work. Helen and friends at the diner chatted as they fussed over the baby. It was a pleasant two hours.

It was a warm evening. Helen decided to take a walk. As she pushed the buggy, she looked in the store windows. She came upon an ice cream shop and went in. She bought a ice cream cone and left. Ron was starting to fuss. He was hungry. Helen headed home as she ate her ice cream.

When she got home, she saw a letter in her mailbox. It was her welfare check. She went upstairs and nursed Ron. After he went asleep, she used the phone in the hall to call the salvation army lady. The salvation army lady told Helen she would come by in a couple days. Then Helen called home. The phone rang many times. No one answered. She would try again later. She didn't know if her parents would talk to her. She had to try.

The next morning, Helen was awakened by Ron's crying. She got up and nursed him. She put him in his crib, took a shower and got dressed. She went into the living room and saw Ron standing up. She went to Ron, picked him up and dressed him, while talking to him.

After her breakfast, she put Ron in the buggy and went to the phone to call home again. She wanted to tell her parents about Ron. After a few rings, her mother answered.

"Hi mom," said Helen. "I called to tell you, you are a grandmother and ask if it might be ok to come home. I miss you and dad."

"I really don't know," mom said. "I would like that, but not sure about your dad. Call me tomorrow and I'll let you know."

"I have some money set aside and a month's check. I am about six months' pregnant. I love you and dad. Ron is starting to fuss. I will call you tomorrow. Bye."

Helen went back to the apartment and changed Ron. As she sat in her rocking chair, holding Ron, she decided to send her parents a picture of her and Ron. She truly wanted to see her parents again. Helen went to Sears to get a picture of her and Ron to send home.

Afterwards, she went to the park. It was a nice, warm day. After a while, she sat on a bench to rest. She had gotten big. She was due in about two months. She hoped to be with her parents when she delivered. Helen walked back to her apartment. It was a long walk and needed to rest again. She turned on the radio, sat down in the rocking chair, and nursed Ron until he fell asleep. She put Ron in his crib and went back to the chair and took a nap. Helen woke up. Ron was still sleeping. She made lunch and ate it. The day passed.

She got up the next morning and changed and nursed Ron. Afterward, she put Ron in his crib. He was standing without holding on. She took him out of the crib and put him on the floor. He had learned how to walk. She was proud as she watched him around the room.

There was a knock on the door. It was the salvation army lady. Her name is Amy. Helen asked her in. They fussed over Ron. Helen told Amy her situation. The woman gave Ron a couple toys she brought with her. The women talked for a long time. Helen didn't tell her about her inheritance. She asked Helen if she needed anything. Helen said eventually she would need clothes for the baby. The woman told her to come to the salvation army store at her convenience and gave her the address and $25 in vouchers.

Shortly after the woman left, Helen went into the hall and called her mom. The phone rang a few times before her mom answered it.

"Hello," said her mom.

"Hi mom," said Helen. "What did dad say?"

"I talked to him till I was blue in the face. He said no. Give him time. Maybe he will change his mind. I have got to go. He is coming into the house. Call again soon. Bye." Mom hung up. Helen had some hope because her mother talked to him. She hung up the phone and went back to her apartment.

Days turned into weeks. Helen's delivery date was getting closer as she got bigger. She called Amy, the salvation army lady, and told her she was about to deliver her baby. Amy made arrangements to take care of Ron when the time came.

A few days later, when Helen was asleep, her water broke. She got up and called Amy. It was very early in the morning and dark outside. Ron was still asleep when Amy arrived at Helen's apartment. She wrapped Ron in a blanket and carried him to the car. Helen was having labor pain. It was August of 1948.

Helen was in labor for a short time. She named the baby Clyde, Jr. He was a small, sickly baby. Helen stayed in the hospital for seven days. Junior stayed in the nursery for 12 days. Helen was glad not to be pregnant and determined to stay that way. Junior required many visits to the clinic. Over time, he became healthier, bigger, and stronger.

A few weeks went by, Helen lost her pregnancy weight and got her figure back. Helen started dating the neighbor's son, Javon. He was the third Mexican she had dated. Both Ron's and Junior's fathers were Mexican. Javon had two sisters. Inga babysat for Helen when she went out with Javon. He had a good paying job as a mechanic and his own car. After dating two Mexican men, Helen read and spoke fluent Spanish.

Javon was a passionate man in his early 20's. The children liked and got along good with him. Helen and Javon spent a lot of time together. He would bring her food from time to time.

The day came when Helen needed to see the doctor. She hoped she was wrong. She thought she might be pregnant again. Javon took her and the children to the clinic. She was really good with the children. The doctor examined the children and Helen. The doctor told her the children were doing well and she was pregnant. Helen was going on 19-years-old and pregnant for the third time. She told herself at least Juan liked children.

On the way home, Helen told Juan she was pregnant. Juan didn't say too much at first. Finally, he asked if she was sure. She told him yes. Juan suggested they start living together. Helen agreed.

Once again, Helen got bigger as the time passed. Juan was a big help. He treated Ron and Junior as his own and Helen like a queen. He couldn't do enough for her.

When Helen's time came to deliver, Juan's sisters watched the children while he took Helen to the hospital. She was glad he was with her. After long hours of labor, Helen gave birth to a girl by c-section. Helen named her Maria. It was September of 1949.

After a short time, Helen and Juan moved to Warsaw, Indiana. After living there for a few months, Helen and Juan started fighting. They would throw food and other things at each other. One time, a pair of scissors was thrown and stuck in the wall above Maria's head. Another time, Junior asked Juan for a drink of his pop. He beat Junior with the bottle. Another time, he hit Junior with a flashlight and knocked two teeth out. Once, while riding in a car, Juan pushed Junior out of the car. One day, Juan wasn't there. It was said he committed a crime for which he was executed.

After that, the family moved to a one-room apartment with a pot belly stove. They all slept on the floor. Helen no longer had public aid benefits. She went to work as a bartender and waitress.

About this time, her new love interest came into her life. He seemed to be scruffy with dirty hair and bad teeth. After a while, Helen, the children and her love interest moved to an apartment with a window looking out to the alley. Ron, Junior, and Maria would drop bricks out the window at the rats. There was a black woman that lived down the hall. She would watch the children while Helen worked. Helen and the woman would leave the doors open so the children could go back and forth. There was a salvation army lady that would come by from time to time and bring the children food and toys. Junior would have bad nightmares about snakes and wake up screaming. The salvation army lady brought Junior a bumblebee toy. She told him if he sleeps with it, he wouldn't have bad dreams. He didn't.

One day, Helen took off. She was gone for a long time. While she was gone, her love interest took care of the children for a while. He would sit on the steps of the building and drink his beer while watching the children play. One time, a neighbor lady caught Junior and her daughter in the closet with their pants down.

After a time, Helen came back. Her love interest left and didn't come back. One day, the salvation army lady came over and took Ron away. Helen could no longer deal with his needs. He went to an orphanage. It was a Christmas day. It was not long after that, Helen gave up Junior to the orphanage. A short time after that, A policeman found Maria sitting on the street curb, while it was 35 degrees outside, wearing just her underpants. She was just 3-years-old. Maria was taken to the orphanage. Soon after that, Helen gave up her parental rights. She did it using an alias. The children didn't see their mother again.

When Helen was gone, the children would throw lit matches at each other. It was a game they played. One day while playing the game, the bedding caught fire and burned down. They were homeless again. The salvation army lady helped to find a new place for them to live. After getting in the orphanage, the children were examined by a doctor. None of the children were potty-trained. Ron had numerous cigarette-burns on his butt and legs. When the doctor took down his pants, he got terrified and screamed. He had to be held down while the doctor treated his injuries. The doctor reassured him he wasn't going to hurt him. Ron passed out from fright. After the doctor was done, he was put in the infirmary, where he stayed for several days.

Junior stuttered so bad he could hardly be understood. He had stomach ulcers. He had difficulty eating without getting sick. He stayed away from people. He too was put in the infirmary. Maria suffers from exposure to the cold, a malnutrition, a want for love and affection, and a severe and bleeding rash from not being potty-trained. She was put in the infirmary.

As time went by, Junior and Maria got better and were put with the other children in the orphanage. Ron was sent to a mental hospital for children for a year. Junior and Maria continuously asked about their brother. They were told he was really sick, but he would be back soon. Junior was sent to the boys' dorm and Maria to the girls' dorm.

After a short time, Junior was put into a foster home. A few months later, he was brought back to the orphanage. The foster parents couldn't deal with his needs. After a very short time, Junior was sent to another foster home. They too returned Junior. They couldn't deal with his needs.

Maria was having a rough time at the orphanage. The director of the girls' dorm was cold and uncompassionate. In the year or so Maria was in the orphanage, she was denied Christmas presents and not allowed to participate in the different functions. She told Maria she was a bad girl and that bad girls didn't get presents and privileges. Maria was having problems getting potty-trained. The one thing that made life bearable for Maria was Mrs. Butler, the case worker at the orphanage. She would bring Maria to her office and spend time with her and give her treats and toys.

At one point, Maria wanted to bring her doll to her dorm, she messed herself and the dorm director took the doll away. She told Maria bad girls can't have dolls. The pastor told Maria, God didn't like bad girls and if she didn't behave, she would not go to heaven. Maria cried.

One day, Mrs. Butler gave Maria a tricycle and frequently brought her to the office so she could play with it. Mrs. Butler would get Ron, Junior, and Maria in her office so they could spend time together. Mrs. Butler would take the three children to get ice cream.

One day, Mrs. Butler took Junior and Maria to her office. There was a man and woman there named Ralph and Jessie. They were 30-years-old and couldn't have children for medical reasons. Mrs. Butler introduced the children to them. After several minutes, Mrs. Butler told the children, Ralph and Jessie wanted to adopt them. The children asked if that included Ron. She said she didn't know, but she would do what she could to make it happen.

After a week or so, Mrs. Butler took Junior and Maria to her office and Ralph and Jessie were there. Mrs. Butler told the children they were going home with them on a trial basis. If it worked out, they would be adopted. Again, the children asked about Ron. Mrs. Butler said she was still working on that but not yet. Mrs. Butler hugged the children, gave Maria her toy she kept in her office, and told the children she would be by to see them from time to time.

On the way to Ralph and Jessie's farm, they stopped for lunch. Junior and Maria had never been to a restaurant before. The waitress gave them menus. Junior told Ralph and Jessie they didn't know how to read. Jessie said that was ok and read the menus to them. Ralph and Jessie knew their work was cut out for them.

After lunch, they went to the farm. As Ralph took the children's things into the house, Jessie took the children by hand and went inside. "Welcome to your new home." Jessie showed the children their rooms. They never had their own rooms before. Jessie helped Maria set up her room and Ralph helped Junior do the same. "How about we take the children exploring." They went outside and showed them the farm.

After a while, as the four of them walked, Junior and Maria were in awe. They asked Ralph and Jessie how many people lived there. Jessie told them, "Just us four." They showed the children the fruit orchard and the fields with vegetables. The orchard had apples and pear trees, as well as strawberry, blueberry and a crabapple tree. Ralph asked the children if they wanted an apple or pear or some berries. They said apples. Ralph was six-feet-four and towered over the children. Jessie was 5-feet-tall. Ralph picked four apples from the tree and gave everybody one. They were delicious. The four of them sat at a picnic table and talked outside while eating their apples. Jessie asked the children if they had any questions.

"Are you rich?" they asked. "Why do you want us? Nobody else wants us. Are you going to give us back to the home, too?" Jessie's eyes teared up. She was moved by their questions. Ralph told the children they could live there for the rest of their lives. They will be family forever. Jessie told the children they could call them mom and dad.

As time went by, the four grew close. Mom and dad taught the children how to read, got Junior help with his stuttering, and got them potty-trained. The family went to church every Sunday. Life was good. Every now and then, Mrs. Butler would bring Ron over to visit, sometimes overnight or on the weekends. Because dad was a professor at Noter dame, he got free tickets to sporting events which he took Junior to. Junior played little league baseball, but wasn't very good at it. Junior excelled more in music and art. Mom taught Maria how to make fruit preserves, can vegetables, and cook in general. Mom was an excellent cook. Maria took ballet lessons. She was very good at it.

The day came when mom, dad, and the two children went in front of the judge. Mom and dad told them it was nothing to be afraid of. He would ask everyone questions and then give a ruling. When the family arrived for court, Mrs. Butler was there. The children asked if she was going to take them back to the home. Mom and dad calmly assured them she wouldn't do that. "She was there to help them all." Mrs. Butler greeted the family with a big smile. The five of them had warm and friendly conversation. The judge came in. The court sat down on the bench.

The bailiff stated, "This court is now in session. The honorable Judge Wilson, presiding." The bailiff read from a paper. "Came this day, Ralph and Jessie to adopt Junior and Maria, both minor children." The judge instructed Jessie to take the children to the hall. She did. The judge questioned Mrs. Butler at length. She told him the children's history. Then the judge told the bailiff to bring back mom and the children. They sat with Ralph and Mrs. Butler. The judge questioned him about his job and ability to support the children and why he wanted to adopt the children. He asked Jessie if she could give the children the love and care, mental and emotional, they needed and deserved. She said yes. He asked her why she wanted to adopt the children. She told him she herself was an orphan and raised in a convent. She knew it was like to not have the warmth and love from a mother and father. The judge then asked mom and dad, knowing the children's history and the many problems, if they both wanted to adopt them. Without hesitation, they both said yes.

He asked the children if they had ever seen a judges' chambers. They said no. He left the bench, walked up to them, and said, "Come with me." The children grabbed mom and dad's hand.

"It's ok," they told the children. "He just wants to talk with you. Just tell him how you feel. Then we can go home." The judge smiled as he reached out his hand. They went into the judges' chambers. The judge pulled up a chair and sat close to them. With a friendly, non-threatening voice, he asked the children if they understood everything happening. Did they know what being adopted meant? Did they have questions or concerns? They answered they were not sure. He asked the children if they wanted to live with Ralph and Jessie and be their son and daughter forever. He asked if they had been treated good and if they had received everything they needed. They said yes. They wanted to know why mom and dad wouldn't let Ron live with them. Maria also told the judge how badly the dorm director treated Ron and her and told him that Mrs. Butler was good to them and let Ron come and visit them and take them to get some ice cream. He took the children back to the courtroom and asked mom and dad and Mrs. Butler to join him in his chambers.

The judge told them the children were wanting to be adopted Ralph and Jessie. They also wanted to know why they would not adopt their brother, Ron. They talked for a long time. Finally, mom, dad, and Mrs. Butler came to the courtroom. A few minutes later, the judge came back in. He sat back at his bench. He said, "From this day on, Junior and Maria will be a son and daughter to Ralph and Jessie and Junior will now be known as Ralph, Jr. Both children will have any and all rights given by law." He went on to say, "I am ordering Ralph, Jessie, and Mrs. Butler to make every effort to allow their brother, Ron, to see and or communicate with Ralph, Jr. and Maria."

"Yes, your honor," replied mom, dad, and Mrs. Butler.

"I am also ordering that abuse claims by Maria committed by the girls' dorm director be investigated. Good luck to you all and congratulations. Court adjourns." The judge came off the bench and shook all their hands. Mrs. Butler congratulated mom, dad, and the children.

All five went to lunch and celebrated. Dad ordered a glass of champagne and two kiddy cocktails for the children. While waiting for their beverages, Mrs. Butler explained that mom and dad tried many times to have Ron come and live with them, but problems ran so deep it wasn't possible at this time. She said that they would continue to work on it and they would make sure the children could see him as often as possible as well as talk on the phone. That made Ralph and Maria feel better. Ralph asked why his name changed. Dad told him he always wanted a son named after him. "Is that ok?"

"Ok," said Ralph. When the beverages came, Mrs. Butler toasted the family and wished them luck and love forever. Dad also toasted stating they were the best children ever. Then dad told the children he sold the farm and was having a brand, new house built. With a big backyard, a swing set, and a slide.

"You children will have a big bedroom each and your own bathroom." After dinner, Mrs. Butler gave the children and mom and dad a big hug and left.

Ralph and his new friend, Jerry, were like brothers. They were in the cub scouts and boy scouts together. Jerry's dad worked at the school. His mom was a nurse. A week after the children's adoption, mom and dad had a big party to introduce them to family and friends. They met dad's sister, Leola, Uncle Quickly and Aunt Irene, and Uncle Nails and Aunt Gurty. All of them were wealthy. Uncle Al and Aunt Lois owned a couple of bar pool halls. The Christianson's were there. They babysat for Ralph and Maria. Grandma and Grandpa

Christianson were elderly. Their two daughters, Maxine and Norma, were both single. Maxine was a good-natured, happy 35-year-old large woman. Norma was a quiet, pleasant thin woman. Ralph had a crush on her. Norma had a bad heart. She passed before the family moved into the new house. She was 30-years-old.

Ralph and Maria were not allowed to go to the service. Mom and dad didn't think it was a good idea considering the situation at the time. By now the children were potty-trained. Ralph had almost stopped stuttering, except when nervous. Both the children had greatly improved. Ralph was in the school band and glee club and sang solos in a few school shows. Maria continued to do well in ballet and baton. All the aunts and uncles gave the children a lot of money. The Christianson's gave each of the children white bibles with their names on them in a gold print. Mom and dad let the children keep a small amount of the money and put the rest in a savings account for them.

After a few months, the family moved into their new home. Mom and the children spent the next few days unpacking. As part of dad's job, he traveled a lot. He went to Africa, India, and Germany to name a few. He participated in the development of the X-15 spacecraft. That Christmas, dad brought home a poodle dog for the family. Mom named it Gigi. Mom got a mink stole from dad. Ralph got a big train set. Maria got a 2-foot-tall doll with a dollhouse. Dad also bought a 2-keyboard electric organ and lessons for the children. They had to practice one half-hour each day. Ralph enjoyed it and practiced 2 hours at a time and became very good at it. When mom and dad had some company over, they would ask Ralph to play. Dad's favorite song was 'I left my heart in San Francisco.' Mom and Maria liked it. Ralph would also play Christmas carols.

One day, a letter came from Mrs. Butler. It said Ron went to live with a family in Ohio and after he got settled with them, she would send them his contact information. A year or so later, she did.

That summer, the family went to Ohio to visit Ron and his family. He was doing much better. It was an enjoyable visit that lasted a week.

At 16-years-old, Maria met Al and started dating him. Al was 30-years-old and divorced. Shortly after Maria and Al started dating, they got married. It took place at a V.P. The church wouldn't allow a divorced person to marry there. Maria was a virgin when she got married and the three days after. Al liked fishing and that is what he did for the first three days.

At 17-years-old, Maria was pregnant with Ronda. Al and Maria moved to Iowa. Al was a good provider. He didn't drink, smoke, or use any drugs. He was cold and unnatural towards Maria.

The day Ronda was born, Al was not happy he had to leave his fishing to drive Maria to the hospital thirty miles away. Ronda was born three weeks before Maria's 18th birthday. Ronda was the only baby in the nursery. It was a small, hick town.

Mom, dad, and Ralph went to Iowa to be there when the baby was born. At this time, Ralph was on leave from the Navy. While in Iowa, Ralph went on a date with a girl he met. During the date, they parked and started making out. As they laid on the back seat, the girl screamed. There were two crawdad's crawling on the back of the seat. It was Al's car. It would seem a can of live bait had spilled over. Ralph's relationship with the girl was short-lived. After a few days, dad had to get back to work and Ralph's leave was coming to an end.

The first few months of her marriage, she slept with some stuffed animals. She wasn't really matured at that time. Maria went home to mom and dad several times during her marriage. The last time, Al told her to stay there. Maria met a man named Pinky. Pinky took Maria to his family farm in Missouri. In the meantime, Ralph married a girl, Judy, because she told him she was pregnant. A week after the wedding, Ralph went back to his duty station. Judy stayed with her mother in Indiana.

A week later, she told Ralph that she wasn't pregnant and that she was sorry about that. Meanwhile, she got all the benefits of a military wife. Ralph's dad told him he had fallen victim to the oldest con in history. Dad talked to a lawyer in Indiana and Ralph talked to a Navy legal officer. They both said the same. Since marriage had been consummated, an annulment wasn't possible, and because he was married in Indiana, he would have to pay alimony if he divorced Judy.

Meanwhile, Pinky's family in Missouri were treating Maria and Ronda cruelly and downright rude. Pinky had left Maria at the farm and took off. Pinky's brother tried to take care of Maria. There was no plumbing or electric in the house. One time during a tornado, the old lady wouldn't let Maria in the storm cellar. Eventually, Pinky came back and took Maria and Ronda to Colorado where he found a job. Maria loved living in Colorado. One day, Maria and Pinky left Colorado to visit mom and dad. The only problem was Pinky stole his boss' car and credit card. Pinky, Maria, and Ronda were picked up in a hick town. The jail was in the sheriff's house. Maria stayed in a cell with the door left open. The sheriff's wife helped Maria as much as she could to take care of the baby. The sheriff told Maria if she paid the charges on the credit card and paid for the car, she would cut her loose. Dad paid the tab for the car and credit card and Maria came home. She never saw Pinky again.

After Maria got a job at Briteway. Mom took care of Ronda while Maria was at work. After sometime passed, dad suggested Maria let Judy watch Ronda because mom had some back-nerve problems. A couple weeks later, Judy started putting the bad mouth on Maria, telling lie after another to dad. He believed them. Dad went on about how good a person and mother Judy was and how bad a mother Maria was. He went to tell her he would let Ralph and Judy adopt Ronda. Maria blew her cookie. She told dad the truth about Judy and went to tell dad he was senile and old. Dad started beating her and calling her awful names. Mom screamed and told Maria's dad to stop. She pulled dad off Maria. Dad threw Maria and Ronda out and told them to never come back or call anymore.

That demand lasted 5 years. When Maria left mom and dad, she moved in with a girlfriend. After a short time, Maria got a two-room apartment. She got a job in a factory and Ronda was put in foster care. She would visit Ronda every day. From time to time they would bring Ronda to Maria's apartment. She and Ronda had a close mother-daughter relationship. There was a bad winter storm and for three days Maria couldn't get over to see Ronda. Maria called the foster family and told them she would get there when the weather broke. At that time, she called the foster family to see Ronda, but she was told she would have to speak to the case worker beforehand. The caseworker informed her Ronda had been moved and that she would never see Ronda again with no explanation why. At the case worker's office, they refused to discuss it with her. Maria picked up a chair and threw it at the woman. As she started to go over the desk after the woman, security subdued her. After that, Maria took up with a local motorcycle group. She wasn't told the worst they had done was dine and dash. They drank a lot, but mostly they would cruise around on their bikes. There was no sex or drug use. They just hung out.

Meantime, Ralph was still married to Judy. By now, Ralph had fathered two children, a boy, Ricky, and a girl, Margaret. On one occasion, mom was in the hospital for illness. The doctors didn't know if she was going to make it. Ralph and Judy were at Maria's apartment talking about mother's health. When Judy made a statement. "I hope the bitch dies." Before Ralph could stop her, Maria started punching Judy with about the force of a punching bag. It took all of Ralph's strength to pull Maria off of her. Judy said she was going to call the police. Ralph told her he saw her trip over her own feet. Ralph wanted to do what Maria did, but he didn't hit women. The police were called and came. Judy almost got arrested for being rude and threatening the police.

After Judy took the children and everything they owned and went home to her mother every Thanksgiving through Christmas, while filing for separation or divorce five times over a six-year period, Ralph and Judy got back together. Eventually, they lived in Chicago. Judy stabbed Ralph and tried to shoot him with his own gun. Fortunately, she was a bad shot. Ralph knew at that point that the marriage was over.

After Ralph's divorce, he entered an apprentice tool and die training job. It didn't go well. After about a year and a half later, the apprenticeship ended. He filed for unemployment and eventually had to give up his apartment due to his cut in income. He moved to Schefield and Irving Park in Chicago, about two blocks from Wrigley field stadium and one block from Lake Michigan beach. The neighborhood was made up of pimps, hookers, drug dealers and junkies. Ralph's apartment was next to the L track station.

Ralph spent his pay at the beach and going to baseball games when he had money for a ticket. When he wasn't doing that, he would sit at a diner or bar, or just walk around the neighborhood. One day, while sitting in a diner, he met a girl named Etna. She was 22 years old and attractive. She was a waitress at the diner. It was love at first sight, but was short-lived. After a month or so, Etna told Ralph her family didn't approve of their relationship. Ralph told her he didn't care, he wanted to be with her. Etna felt the same about Ralph.

A few days later, two large black men came into the diner where Ralph and Etna were sitting together. Etna got upset. She told Ralph they were her two older brothers. Before Ralph could say anything, the two men were at the table. One of them told Etna to leave the table. Etna refused. The man told Etna if she didn't, Ralph could have a bad accident. "You need to stay within your own race," the man said. Etna said she loved Ralph and that race didn't matter. Ralph agreed. One of the men got behind Ralph and said, "Last chance," as he grabbed his neck and pulled him out of his chair. Etna screamed for them to stop.

"Stop, stop, stop!" Etna said. She walked over to Ralph and told him she loved him too much to see him hurt and could no longer be with him. The man let Ralph loose and Etna and the two men left the diner. Etna was in tears. Ralph fell back in his chair gasping for air. While holding his throat, a small, older man in an apron and paper hat walked up to him.

"Are you going to be ok?" the man said.

"I think so," Ralph said. "I still want to be with her."

"Is she worth dying over?"

"Yes!" he said. Ralph came back to the diner a number of times, but he never saw her again. Ralph moved on. It took him a long time to get over Etna.

A couple of hookers befriended Ralph. Dee and Barb were both good looking, good natured women. When the women weren't working, the three spent a lot of time together. Ralph received a notice his unemployment was about to end. As the three sat in the bar talking, Ralph

mentioned it. The women suggested Ralph move in with them and be their bail man. Dee told

him she had four women on her string. All he had to do was be there when they needed him and

bail them out of jail if they got pinched. In exchange, he would get a place to live, meals, all the

sex he wanted, and $100 a day from each woman. Ralph agreed.

Life was good. He had all the money he needed. The women didn't get pinched all that

often. The only inconvenience was that Ralph had to stay out of the way when the women

worked the street corner.

As she waited for the light to change, a car pulled up, a shotgun came out of the

passenger window and emptied both barrels into Barb and sped away. Dee and Ralph ran out of

the diner to the street corner. Barb was dead. A crowd had gathered and the police were starting

to arrive. Ralph told Dee they had to leave and they walked away from the corner. As they

walked back to the apartment, Dee told Ralph the police would write a report, but because of

how dark it was and that she was a hooker, nothing would be done about the shooting. Ralph

asked if they should claim the body.

"No. If we do it, it would bring unwanted attention to us."

A short time after that, Ralph took his money, bid farewell to Dee and moved from the

neighborhood. He got an apartment on the north side in a better neighborhood. He got a job

paying union wages at a non-union fastener factory. At Christmas time, the factory had a big

Christmas party and dinner dance for the employees. Ralph had a date for the party, but got stood

up. He went to the party anyway. As he sat at the table, the waitress brought the meals. He paid

for two meals, but the waitress only brought one. Ralph told the waitress she was one short. He told her his date was invisible and she should bring the second meal and she did. While at the party, Ralph met his future wife. She was young and attractive. The two had a good time at the party. A few months later, they were married. She was 18 years old and him, 29. Ralph fathered two children in that marriage, a son and a daughter. His son went on to a successful military career. His daughter became a published writer in her junior year of high school and received a bachelor degree from a Wisconsin university. Both children married and gave Ralph and his wife three grandchildren. Ralph's son from his first marriage gave him a grandson. That son went on to start a successful business. At this time, Ralph and his wife have been married near forty years.

Meantime, Maria remarried, had two more children and got married again. Her last husband died from brain cancer. Maria's children gave her six grandchildren. One is an athlete. Another is a registered nurse. These days Maria is the guardian to one of her grandchildren and that keeps her busy the majority of the time.

Today, Ralph, his wife, and Maria are retired, senior citizens. Ralph does volunteer work. His wife takes care of their grandchildren while their son serves in the military and goes to school to be a physician's assistant. Neither Maria nor Ralph have heard from Ron in over 45 years.